From Sinner to Saint: Clawing Up to Heaven

Albert Oon

ISBN: 9798688492675

SHORT STORIES WITH EXTRAS

Saint within the Sinner
Albert Oon

"The good man though a slave, is free; the wicked, though he reigns is a slave" – St. Augustine

Chapter 1 – Devil-Possessed Prisoner

When a person sins, they open themselves up to demons. The demons use this opportunity to make the sinner sin more and in harsher ways. In this world, the demons sometimes manifest themselves through the person. The sinners think that they are given a special power over them when, in fact, the demons are just using them as their puppet, and the more a person sins, the more a person loses themselves. The Church's division of exorcists is busier than ever because of this as the demons that use gullible and prideful sinners to commit evil deeds while staying as far away from them as possible.

There are three levels of demonic possession. Disruptors are people who experience slight demonic possession, but mostly have control of themselves and know that they should seek immediate help. Hallucinated are people who think their abilities are natural or a gift from God that they are just learning how to control. These kinds of people can recognize that the condition they have is bad only when they sin in a way they didn't intend. The last and most dangerous level is keter. These people are sinners convinced that they have control over the demons possessing them and use them to do whatever they want or whatever the demons suggest. Keter level possession wipes a person's memory of who they are and restricts them to a barebones moral compass. People with the keter level possession are actively sought out after by the Church who go to extreme lengths to capture and contain them.

Currently, there is an escorted prison carriage carrying a keter level possessed woman to the nearest demon treatment facility. Her name is Estella and she's been a high priority target who's been causing trouble in the area for months with her prostitution ring. In the carriage with her is a nun who is constantly mentally praying with her eyes closed to suppress Estella's demonic power.

"What's that red cross on your head, sister? Does it mark you as someone special?" Estella asks.

"..."

"You must be if so many people were dedicated to protecting you. What makes you special?"

"..."

"Does it have to do something with your eyeshadow? I thought nuns weren't supposed to wear makeup. You look like one of my girls now that I have a good look at you."

"..."

Aggravated by the nun's silence, Estella's demon of persuasion manifests from her eye.

"You know all your people died painfully because of me, my girls, and goons. I made sure you witnessed every second of it to break you down so if we won, you would be easier to turn into another willing toy to sell for a man's pleasure."

The nun opens her eyes with a disgusted look on her face. Estella mischievously grins as she eagerly awaits her response before being stabbed in the eye with a crucifix dagger that makes the demon dematerialize.

"Agh! You! You're lucky that my eye heals, and I'm restrained."

"Silence, whore," the nun says with a stern voice that only further aggravates Estella.

"Do you think that my friends will just let you take me away? I'm too valuable for them to just let go."

"They can't save you. Only God can. You should be thanking us for bringing you to a place where you're going to be healed."

"You don't think my powers are a gift from God? They're a reward for providing an essential service to lonely people who need to feel a sense of closeness to others."

"You make people into mindless slaves of pleasure."

"Haha, call it what you want. I do what I'm supposed to." The prison carriage is abruptly attacked by Estella's supporters. "My friends have arrived. Beg for mercy now and I'll ease you into your new role."

The nun goes back to her prayers and tries to concentrate despite the action and the rocking of the carriage.

"Your prayers won't help you, sister! This is God's will that you become mine!"

The fighting outside shakes the carriage in a way that makes the nun fall on Estella's lap. With this opportunity, Estella's demon comes out from her eye and a hand materializes from her stomach. The demon's hand holds the nun's throat as the demon speaks through Estella.

"Submit to me before it's too late," it says before chanting a spell on her.

The nun manages to break free of the trance and uses her crucifix dagger to stab Estella in the eye again. This dematerializes the demon's head and hand.

"Agh! Stop doing that!"

"I'll stop if you stop being such a filthy wretch!"

The carriage then flips over and breaks. Estella and the nun aren't seriously injured by the crash as both make it to their feet, however, Estella's demons make her get on her feet faster so she can escape. Once she escapes, she finds that both her rescue and the Church's escort have been killed to the last man.

"Guess I'll have to make my own way back."

Estella's demons manifest from her eye and stomach to try to break her bonds but can't manage it. Even her strengthened arms aren't able to do anything to them.

Meanwhile, the nun manages to sneak up behind her and stab her crucifix dagger into her stomach.

"AAAAH!! You…"

The nun says a prayer while turning the dagger like a key until the prayer is done. She takes out the dagger and slowly walks away from Estella. Estella gets up and turns to the nun with a gentle smile.

"Sister Astra. What's the matter?" Estella asks.

"You said that name the first time we gave you a minor exorcism. How do you know my name?"

"I don't know. I just somehow recognize your face, and what do you mean minor exorcism? Can't you fully exorcise these demons from me?"

"I don't have the authority to even though I'm a Supreme Moderator nun. That's why we have to hurry before you lose control again."

"I won't lose control again. I promise. I'll do whatever I'm supposed to."

From Sinner to Saint: Clawing Up to Heaven

"Don't make promises you can't keep. Sinners like you typically fall into your filth over and over again without much or any resistance to it."

"Why did you have to say that, Astra? It won't help me stay in control."

"Because it's the truth. You and so many others have done it before, and you'll do it again if the demons aren't exorcised from you."

"Okay…I understand."

"We'll be blessed if a patrol of exorcists finds us. It'd be easier to get you to the closest demon treatment facility. What are you waiting for? Follow me."

"Ye-yes, Astra."

"Stop calling me by my first name and just call me sister."

"Yes, sister."

Astra and Estella make their way through the wreckage of the failed rescue attempt and follow the road in the hopes of it leading to a nearby town or place to rest.

Meanwhile, Estella's demons that are sparked by Estella's annoyance of Astra's harshness slowly regain their energy and wait for the right opportunity to strike.

Chapter 2 – Piety and Pretentious

While walking along the road, Astra continues silently praying and Estella tries to not be bored.

Unable to take it anymore, Estella asks, "Do you know this road, sister?"

"…"

"If you do, do you know how much longer it will take to get to the nearest town?"

"…"

"If you are too caught up in your prayers to talk to me, then can you at least pray for me? I'm afraid that I'm feeling impatient and…something else."

"Don't go proving me right."

"I'm trying not to. Hey, don't you think it might be safer to go through the woods? There are probably more people after me and they might be using the roads."

"And you don't think that the woods are dangerous?"

"Well…they might be, but I don't know."

"Just don't worry about it and stop bothering me."

"Can you at least tell me why I'm so irritating to you?"

"…"

"Is it something personal? I feel like it's something personal as if you were in my position before."

"You really need to be questioned once you get your memories back."

"Am I correct?"

"What did I say before?"

"I understand, sister."

"She's a danger to you," a demon says inside Estella's head.

"No, you are," Estella responds inside her head.

"I can grant you safety and a good life. You remember how good you had it before."

"But that was…wrong. It wasn't me."

"It was you. No one else could do the job you were doing. It was your God-given role."

"I don't think you would know anything about that."

"And the nun does? You can smell her pride. Her sins reek more horribly than yours. You know her past. She's no nun."

"I'm not going to listen to you anymore."

"Why? I've been your trusted advisor. Kill the nun before she can bring you to the exorcists. Do you think the tattoos on your eye, arms, and stomach will be painlessly removed? The pain that your penance requires will be severe."

"If that's what I'll have to do to get rid of you, I'll…"

"Will you go through it? I don't think you want to. I don't think that you're the most sinful one here. She is. Kill her."

The demon repeatedly commands Estella to kill Astra in a trance-like manner that makes Estella move behind Astra with the intent to kill her. Her demons come out of her stomach, eye, and struggle to come out of their restraints as they thirst for blood.

"No, no! I don't want to kill her. You can't make me! What was that prayer that the nun said before?"

From Sinner to Saint: Clawing Up to Heaven

"You don't have the authority to say it to us," a demon says.

"I think I do."

Estella says the nun's prayer in her head and the demons recede for now. She then walks into Estella as she regains full control of herself.

"Watch where you're going. We're here," Astra says in an annoyed tone after slapping Estella.

"Huh? Oh."

Astra and Estella see that they've arrived in a small town.

"It's a good thing we managed to find this place so quickly."

"If you say so. This is a relatively uninteresting place with inns and places to stock up on food, drink, and basic weapons for self-defensc on the dangerous roads. It's not really a good place to make a living."

"Still, it's a good thing it's here."

Right now is the time of day when businesses start packing up and the night workers come in. When they see Estella entering the town, the people who have things to give go to her and offer them to her while others ask what she needs.

"Huh? What's all this for? What did I do?" Estella asks.

The people are confused about her response and whisper to themselves.

"I'm sure it has something to do with that sinfully wretched side of yours and whatever she did. People of this humble town, you have nothing to fear from this whore because I have restrained her demons and am taking to a place where she can be freed from her wicked nature and will do penance for her evil deeds."

The people of the town rejoice and profusely thank Astra. She soaks in the praise while telling them that she doesn't need it. While Astra is distracted by the crowd,

From Sinner to Saint: Clawing Up to Heaven

Estella looks around then notices a tattooed man on a horse arriving in the town. He asks the people around the town questions and Estella assumes that he's asking about her.

"Sister, I think we have trouble."

"Trouble? What trouble could there be with all of these great people here?"

"Look over there. I think that tattooed man is looking for me."

"Huh? Oh. He does look like trouble."

"Uh oh. I think he's noticed us."

"Sorry, grateful citizen, but we have to leave!"

Astra and Estella try to make a quick escape from the crowd and hide, but they are quickly caught up to by the tattooed man who finds them when they turn a corner.

"Estella! I knew I would find you here at one of our favorite places to relax and find more workers!" the man says with a sinister grin.

"I don't know who you are! Leave us alone!"

"What? But I'm your favorite! You tell me every time we…you! You whore of a nun! What did you do to my mistress?!"

Demons with blades coming out of their mouth manifest themselves in the tattooed man's eyes and mouth.

"I exorcised her and brought her back to her senses! The same thing that I'm going to do to you!" Astra says before starting her exorcism prayer.

The prayer appears to be ineffective as the man charges at her and knocks her down.

"You don't have any help to constrain me like you did my mistress. There's a reason I'm her favorite and I'm going to show it to you!"

"No, stop!" Estella says as she pushes the man away from Astra.

"You shouldn't get in the way, my mistress. I don't want to hurt you."

"If you don't want to hurt me, then leave me alone! I order you to!"

"I'm sorry but I can't do that. I have to bring you back and help you get back to the way you were. You helped me when no one else will. You gave me a place I can call home and people I can call family! I need you to come back home!"

"No!"

Demons come out of Estella's eye, stomach, and her arm restraints are broken by a demon within her arms.

"Don't use the power of your demons, Estella! You'll completely lose control!"

"I-I can handle it. I can control it. There's no other way for us to get out of this. I have to do what I can."

Estella attacks the tattooed man with her demons and slashes at him her tattooed hand, but he doesn't do anything.

"That nun and her friends have weakened you despite your exquisite tattoos. I've taken harsher beatings from you in the past."

Aggravated by her ineptitude, the demon in her eye bites off half the man's head though it doesn't appear to be over just yet as he smiles.

"Haha, that's the Estella I remember."

Estella then gets pushed back as a demon head with other demons coming out of it manifest from half the man's head.

"I got the inside of my mouth tattooed just in case anything like this happened. What do you think?"

"I think you're giving me an even better reason to kill you."

Estella's anger gets to her and the demons give her more power. Seeing this, the tattooed man's demons take away his powers so that Estella can critically wound him and cut his body in half with her claw-like hands.

From Sinner to Saint: Clawing Up to Heaven

"I-I'm glad I brought you back-"

Estella crushes the tattooed man's head into mush with the demon hand in her stomach. She is then ominously quiet as she tries to stand still while shaking.

"Estella?" Astra says as she cautiously approaches Estella with her crucifix dagger drawn.

With her back bent completely backward, Estella says with a smile, "Yes, sister?"

"I knew this would happen! People like you never listen to me!"

"I did what I had to do while you were no help at all." Estella straightens herself out as she turns around as she struggles to regain control of her fading true self. "You…you're nothing to me, sister Astra. Never were. Always an annoyance. Always took the spotlight away from me."

"What are you talking about? I don't have a clue as to who you were before."

Estella charges forward and puts Astra's face into the dirt.

"Bow before your superior…superior…mother."

Flashes of her old memory wake up Estella and give her the strength to say an exorcism prayer to regain some control of herself. The demons inside her fight to stay in control as they make her run away into the woods. Astra gets up and wonders what Estella was talking about.

A citizen of the town approaches Astra and asks, "Aren't you going to go after her?"

"I had a hard enough time restraining her the first time, and I had help that time. This time. It's impossible."

"But isn't anything possible with God?"

"Yes, but I can't do anything."

"Why don't you ask God for help?"

"You don't think I do already?"

"No, but maybe you have to pray harder. It seems like she's struggling to control herself so you could use that to help you exorcise the demons from her."

"Hmmm. You have a point."

"So, are you going to go after her?"

"…yes, I will."

Astra heads off after Estella while leaving the kind citizen without a thank you for their helpful advice.

Chapter 3 - Knowledge from a fellow sinner

Estella struggles to control herself as she prays to lessen the demons' power over her. After a while of praying, the demons lose their grip on her and she regains control of herself. Seeing that she's alone in the woods, she waits and looks around for Astra.

"Astra!" she calls out.

"She isn't coming for you," a demon in her mind says.

Instead of talking back to the demon, Estella continues mentally praying while also ignoring their voices.

From Sinner to Saint: Clawing Up to Heaven

"Astra! Sister! I'm in control of myself again! I swear!"

"Who would risk their life to save a whore like you?"

The continuous chatter of the demon's in Estella's mind starts to worry her so she walks faster back to the town in the hopes of finding Astra. While retracing her steps, Estella hears the sound of moaning in the distance. Not knowing if this is Astra or not she makes her way to it to find a grey tree with four branches on it with eye-like marks on them. The tree's roots are visible as if they were feet and the leaves on the branches seem to be fingers. What's also strange about the tree is that the other trees are further away from it as if they all moved away from it. Another strange thing about it is how the bark of the tree feels like human skin. Estella can't help but be intrigued by the tree and notice all these things about it.

Cracks within the tree then begin to expand and appear to form large faces with eyes, noses, and mouths that mumble to themselves. The branches of the tree then begin to move like arms and the roots begin to move like feet stuck in the ground. It takes a second for this to register to Estella because of how strange it is, but when it does, she screams, trips, and falls on the ground.

"Wait, don't run away. Please, don't be afraid of me," a deep voice says from the largest face on the tree.

"Why should I?"

"I can't do anything to you and I'm a priest."

"Huh. I wouldn't imagine a priest to look like a living tree."

"I apologize for my appearance, but it's the penance I must pay for my sins."

"What did you do?"

"I wanted to be perfect in every way for God. Demons tempted me and I gave in to them by sinning in every way that I could think of to experience sin so I know what every sin feels like so I would know how to counter it. What I blinded myself to was that I was killing my soul to an almost immeasurable degree."

"How could you not know that you were doing the wrong thing?"

"The demons preyed on my pride as a pious man. I also involved my family and friends with my sins, and they join me in my penance, as a result. You look like the way I did when I first started my evil quest for perfection. Don't repeat the same mistake I did because this is how you may turn out in the end."

"I'm trying not to. Is there anyway I can help you?"

"Pray for me."

"Is that all I can do? What about cutting you down?"

"Please don't. If you do, I'll suffer more pain in Purgatory."

"If you say so."

"Thank you. I sense a nun in the woods. She is coming for you."

"I know her! How do you know all that?"

"God has allowed me this ability to help lost people in the woods. If I can help you, then my penance is lessened."

"Can you tell me anything else about her? She seems to really hate me."

"What I can tell you is that you are part of the reason she is the way she is right now. You put that red cross on her forehead. You taught her everything she knows and practices."

"Really?"

"Yes, and if she knew who you really were, then her tone would completely change with you. Unfortunately, that's all that I'm allowed to know about your relationship with her but telling her what I told you will make it clear to her who you were.”

“Thank you so much! You’ll always be in my prayers! Which way is Astra? The nun?”

The tree points forward and Estella heads in that direction after saying goodbye and giving him a hug. Estella runs in the direction of Astra while calling out to her.

“That’s Estella,” Astra says with her crucifix dagger drawn.

Estella finds Astra and holds up her hands.

“It’s me, Astra! Don’t worry about me! I’m in control of myself!”

“Nice try, demon, but I don’t believe you.”

“No, I’m really in control! I used the prayers you said to suppress the power of the demons over me.”

“Impossible. You have to have high authority in the Church to use them.”

"What if I do? A priest who's a tree told me that I put the red cross on your forehead and taught you everything that you know and practice."

Astra is surprised by what Estella says and lowers her guard for a second before putting it back up.

"That's impossible!"

"I don't think it is. I was remembering something about a superior and a mother. I'm not your mother, am I?"

"…no."

"Well, what else could I be? Maybe…maybe you should stab me with the dagger again and say the prayer to further release the demons' power over me. I'll do whatever I'm supposed to so that-"

"Stop saying that!"

"Saying what?"

"That you'll do whatever you're supposed to!"

"Why? What's wrong with that?"

"Because that's what my Mother Superior always used to say!"

"Is that who I was?"

"You can't be! It's impossible! You may share her name and her saying, but your looks and mannerisms are nothing like hers."

"I'll bring you to the priest who's a tree."

"Fine."

Estella brings Astra to the priest who comes to life when they approach him.

"So, you're the priest that Estella was talking about. I've heard stories about you but didn't believe them."

"It's a pleasure to meet you, sister. Please, keep me in your prayers."

"Sure. Hold on a second." Astra takes out her crucifix dagger and tries to stab the tree, but her dagger can't pierce its skin. "You are holy, aren't you? I'm sorry for having doubts. I just can't believe what I was being told."

"Why is that?"

"First of all, she said it came from a talking tree who was a priest. Second, my Mother Superior was a pious woman who mysteriously disappeared one day without a trace and Estella here looks and acts nothing like I remember, especially when the tattooed man we faced not too long ago mentioned that she took him in. She rejected me when I first was brought to the convent because I was a thrown away prostitute that was saved by a sister in the convent."

"I did?" Estella asks.

"She is your long lost Mother Superior. You know now that the source of this information is holy, so release yourself from your doubts and accept it."

"I still feel like I can't."

"Your stubbornness and pride are going to be your undoing just as it was Estella's undoing."

"What are you talking about? She would never fall to any sin."

"Everyone falls to sin especially the uptight and overly pious. Estella was kidnapped by the people she would rule over and tricked into becoming the person she is today. She was told in order to do what God wanted her to do in life, she had to submit herself to her kidnappers, or else she would fail God and die. Unable to let her pride go, she fell to sin and turned into what you see before you."

"This is so unbelievable to me."

"Is it really? She became what you were while you became what she was. Even though I don't know what God intends with the both of you, it seems as if He put you in the other's place to make you learn how the other feels. One was once a self-righteous nun now made a common whore and the other was a common whore made into a self-righteous nun."

"Tch. I guess it makes sense."

Astra looks at Estella who looks back at her with concern and guilt in her eyes.

"I'm sorry for making you stand out so much and for treating you so badly," Estella confesses.

"I'm sorry for-for not completely believing this is you. We still need to perform an exorcism for you so you can have all your memories, and this perverted appearance and personality can be erased. You can apologize when you remember everything that you're sorry for."

"Come on. Can't you just show a little affection?"

Estella offers a hug with her arms out, but Astra turns away from her.

"Don't make me doubt you more. The Mother Superior I knew hardly showed any kind of affection."

From Sinner to Saint: Clawing Up to Heaven

"You two should be on the move. Estella's followers are still after her and they just entered the woods after finding the body of the man you killed. I would fight them off for you, but my current form doesn't allow it," the priest says.

Estella thanks the priest as they leave while Astra stays silent as she leads them away. They aren't fast enough to make it to any kind of safety as Estella's followers catch up to her.

"We're here to bring you back to your castle, my mistress," they say.

"My queen."

"My loving mother."

"You can drop the act of pretending to be on her side. Ask and we'll do anything you want to her."

"I want you to leave us alone!" Estella commands.

"We can't do that for you."

"The nun still has her control over her."

"We'll bring you back to your senses."

"If you're not going to listen to me…"

"Don't use the power of the demons inside you,"

Astra says to Estella.

"I won't though I don't like our odds of escaping."

"We'll have to make it somehow."

Astra and Estella fight to escape Estella's followers, but aren't able to do much since Estella's followers use the power of their demons to overwhelm them. The demons feed on the fear of Astra and Estella who gave into their fear rather than trust in God. As a result, they are knocked out and brought back to Estella's castle.

Chapter 4 – Desperation and Renewal

Astra wakes up in a daze in a cell room with a bed and dresser. The room has a strong stink to it and appears to be a room a prostitute would live in. She sees that one of her arms is chained to the side of the wall and her clothes are torn to shreds. With her senses coming back to her, she sees that her legs and her left arm have been cut off and tattooed for demonic possession. All these things that she sees make her feel enraged, desperate, and distressed at the same time.

She bangs on the cell wall and writhes in the bed as she tries to escape somehow. After a few minutes of this futile escape attempt, the words for cursing her captors and Estella come to her mouth but are stopped as soon as Estella enters the room. Somewhat relieved by this, she ceases the thoughts to curse or hate anyone as Estella rushes to her side.

"Astra! Are you okay?" she asks.

"I don't know. My body feels numb and my nerves feel unhinged. How did you get them to let you go?"

"I…I do what I had to."

"…of course you did."

"I'm sorry, but I had no other choice."

"Of course you had a choice!"

"I know, but I was too weak to make it."

"Then watch me make the right choice when they give it to me."

"I don't think they'll let you."

"What?"

"They might've already…umm."

"What? What did they do to me that could be worse than all of this?"

"Don't worry about that. What you need to worry about is what they'll do after. Actually, no. Just worry about praying. I'll try to do whatever I can to free you."

"I've tried praying and this is where it led me."

"Astra, don't say that. You're supposed to be a strong pious nun, right? That's what I trained you to be."

"And this is what it's made us into! Maybe I should make the same decisions you did for both our sakes."

"No, Astra! You have to choose to be better!"

"Shut up! What do you know about being better?!"

Demons start to manifest from the tattoos on Astra's severed arm and legs. A giant demon head manifests from Astra's arm while two demon mouths with blade-like tongues manifest from her legs. The demons whisper in her ear on what to do to obtain her freedom while complimenting her devotion to God and how holy she is.

"You have to stop now! Control yourself!"

"I know more about that you filthy whore!"

Astra uses the demon on her arm to free her other arm. She then smacks Estella against the wall with it and breaks open her cell door.

"Astra…wait…"

"I'll show you true piety. I'll become an even better person than you ever were by destroying every sinner in this Godforsaken place."

As Astra heads off to kill everyone in the building, Estella struggles to get up.

"I'm sorry, God, for being such a failure of a teacher to Astra. Please, give me the strength to fix my wrongs and become the person I was meant to be."

Estella's prayer is answered almost immediately as her strength comes back to her. She gets up and goes to the place where they are keeping Astra's crucifix dagger.

Meanwhile, Astra slaughters everyone who she comes

across, even the slaves who she deems too sinful to live.

Estella tries to ignore the screams and sounds of fighting

while going to the right room. There she finds the crucifix

dagger.

"Are you sure you can do this?" a demon whispers

in her ears.

"You are no longer Mother Superior," another

points out.

"God has long abandoned you to your pride and

lust. Astra will turn into what you are," yet another says.

"We'll see about that," Estella says as she stabs the

crucifix dagger into her tattooed eye, stomach, and arms

while saying an exorcism prayer.

This silences the voices of the demons and gives

Estella some confidence.

"Thank you, God," Estella says while crossing herself and heading in Astra's direction.

Astra has left a massacre of torn bodies in her path with blood and body parts everywhere. Everything from pieces of the wall, ceiling, and furniture have been used to flatten, crush, and tear apart whoever Astra deemed to be a sinner. Eventually, Estella finds Astra in a room filled with chains and the bodies of her victims stomping a body into pulp.

"Astra!"

"You!" Astra says as she quickly turns around, "What do you want, 'Mother Superior'?!"

"I want you to stop this! Don't let your demons take advantage of your weakness."

"I don't have any weaknesses! I'm perfect the way I am!"

"Would a perfect person kill both the innocent and guilty? Look at what you've done."

"Shut up! You're just like them and you'll end up the same!"

"God give me strength."

Estella dodges Astra's incoming attacks while chaining her neck and limbs with the chains in the room all the while loudly saying an exorcism prayer. She then uses the crucifix dagger on Astra's arm demon then the two demons on her legs. Estella's prayer and faith severally weaken the strength of the demons and this allows her to make them disappear and bring Astra to her senses.

"There we go. You should be back to normal for now," Estella says while heavily breathing because of the fight.

Astra starts to sob and cry as she writhes in her chains. Estella hugs her to calm her down.

"I felt the same when it first happened to me too, Astra. I felt irredeemable and used every excuse I could to justify my actions. We're both sinners who need to do a lot of penance for what we've done, and I'll be with you it through it all. Trust in God and me. We'll become saints together."

Astra's crying stops as she puts her head on Estella's shoulder. Estella then frees Astra from her chains and carries her to the horse stables. From there, they leave the building and head in the direction of the nearest demon treatment facility. Thankfully, they come across a patrol of exorcists who guide them to the facility where they are treated. Over the next few days, they recover from their demonic possession and regain themselves and cleanse themselves of their sins.

On one morning, Astra uses her wheelchair made for her condition to visit Estella in her room. Estella has both of her arms in casts, patches on her stomach, and an eye patch for her eye.

"How are you doing, Mother Superior?" Astra asks.

From Sinner to Saint: Clawing Up to Heaven

"Haha, I'm doing fine. You don't have to call me that, Astra. I don't officially have that position in the Church anymore."

"You can be if you come back to the convent."

"That's not going to happen for a while especially in our condition. Did they fix that eyeshadow problem you have?"

"Unfortunately, no. I guess I'll have to carry this scar from my past for the rest of my life along with the rest of my scars. Did they fix your hair problem? It's still pink."

"I don't know I think I like it this way. Haha!"

"You definitely aren't coming back to the convent then."

The two women laugh as they begin their day anew as they put their past behind them for a bright future that lays ahead of them.

The End

Behind the Story

- I have to admit that Estella's outfit on the cover looks weird and a little confusing. Her pants are extremely low to her hip. Any lower and it would be too revealing as if her outfit isn't already revealing enough.

- Astra and Estella's past history is meant to be shown in the way they act. Both are supposed to be acting nearly the same as the other did the last time they were with one another.

- The idea of demons manifesting from tattoos comes from the fact that bad and sinful tattoos can have negative consequences on your spiritual life and can cause you to sin.

- Demons manifesting from your body is a part of this story to add a body horror element to it to emphasize the horror of sin.

- The most dangerous level of possession being

From Sinner to Saint: Clawing Up to Heaven

called keter is a reference to the SCP Foundation, which is a fictional organization that is a web-based collaborative-fiction project with keter being the highest danger level.

- The part about people losing themselves due to sin is inspired by the fact that sin corrupts people from God's original intentions for them.

- Estella's name means "star" while Astra's name means "from the stars".

Albert Oon
Sin or Humanity

Chapter 1 – Infected by Sin

Life is hard and following a strict code of morality makes it even harder. That's why I keep my mind only on the good things in life. What's more important than living a comfortable life and leaving a mark on the world? I may work in a simple coffee shop and live in an apartment, but I have my goals are set on a higher place than this. I won't be conventional about my method nor dirty about it. I won't waste my money on college and I'm not going to work with the cards I've been dealt. What I'm going to do is look for the perfect person to be with and live my life with them.

Because so many people come to the coffee shop I work at, I'm able to look at dozens of men and see if they're the right one for me. If I see one that I like, I spend time with them and try to get them to come back or at least give me their number. The thing about men is that the most handsome and cutest ones can also be the ones who are the fullest of themselves because they know how good-looking they are. I try to ignore those men, but I do fall for them every now and then. My sights are primarily set on the men who don't just look good. They have to radiate confidence and success. Not many men fit my criteria, and you could say that I'm too picky, however, I think I've found the man of my dreams.

His name is Giovane. He's both a writer and a cook. The restaurant he works at isn't anything too impressive, but he makes his food in such a way that his boss lets him add things to the menu. His dishes give the restaurant its great reputation and keep the customers returning and bringing in new ones. He has a small audience of readers and fellow writers. Even though he just has local fame, he does have a growing influence on the world. The only thing that's stopping him from becoming richer and more influential is his eyepatch and scar on his chest.

There are people called "gluttonous sinners" and they hide their deformities with patches and prosthetic body parts. They're called gluttonous sinners because they can never be satisfied with the sin they feed on or something like that. Even though these people are very real because of the attention the Church and government give them, I'm not worried about them. They don't bother me, and I don't bother them, so I don't really care. Sure, there are stories of these sinners turning normal people into them with their bites, but that only happens to gullible people and people who are in the wrong places at the wrong time of day. The part of the city I live in has no confirmed cases whatsoever, so I have nothing to worry about despite what the world news says.

Tomorrow, I'm going on a date with Giovane and I'm trying to shop for a new pair of clothes and shoes for the date, but I keep hearing the latest news on the gluttonous sinners and activity related to them and what we're supposed to do if we are one or if we know someone who is one. I get it that it's important for people to know. I'd just rather not hear about it in almost every place that I go to. Anyway, there isn't here that I think Giovane would find too eye-catching. It's not that I don't already have nice clothes at home. I just want something really special to wow him. What I'm already wearing is already wowing some of the men around me, and it's not even revealing. This tells me that tonight is going to be good.

When the day comes, I wait at the entrance of the coffee shop after work. While waiting, I catch the attention of a few men that usually come to the coffee shop. They're surprised to see me in such a cute outfit, and we talk for a bit. There's no harm in having backups in case Giovane doesn't end up being the one I want. A few minutes after they leave, Giovane meets up with me on time. I hold his arm as we walk and talk through the city.

We go to a fancy restaurant in a skyscraper. Giovane reserved us a couple's spot so we can look down at the city together and by ourselves. Despite the nice setting, I can't help but feel out of place. Mainly rich and upper-middle-class people eat in the restaurant and their dresses and outfits look so much better than ours. We're not underdressed though there's an obvious difference if you have the eye for it.

"Is something on your mind, Lilith?" Giovane asks.

"Oh, no. There sure are a lot of rich people here in this restaurant."

"Not that many people can afford to eat here. Thankfully, people know me in the local cooking business, so they gave me these seats at a good price."

"That's great. I still feel out of place."

"You shouldn't worry about it. People like them can be too judgmental about appearances."

"Do you think you'll ever work your way up to a restaurant like this or one that you'll own by yourself?"

"It's not something that concerns me. I'm happy where I am. Besides, having all that money and responsibility ruins people."

Honest and humble. I'd rather not have any worries about money, but I can imagine living in the upper-middle class. It's better than where I am now.

"I'd like to have the same attitude you have, especially with how much discrimination you must get for your scar and eyepatch."

From Sinner to Saint: Clawing Up to Heaven

"It's worse than what you saw in the coffee shop though I feel more pity than anger. It must suck being paranoid about the people around you all the time."

"I know, but that's the way the world is. I never stop hearing about gluttonous sinners wherever I go."

"Then how about we go somewhere you don't hear about it?"

After we eat, Giovane drives me to a nearby town not too far from the city. It's a nice and quiet place with plenty of humble shops with pretty outfits and dresses that I can't take my eyes off. Around the town, I see other women wearing these outfits. It was one thing that I saw rich people wearing expensive dresses, and now I'm watching lower-middle-class people wearing beautiful dresses that are not as expensive but look better than anything that I have. I try on these outfits just to see what I would look in them.

"You look stunning," Giovane says.

"You think so?"

"Yes, so much so that I'll buy whatever outfits that you want."

"Are you serious?"

"Yes. It's why I brought you here. I didn't exactly know what to get you and you talk a lot about outfits and dresses, so I took you here so I could get you whatever you wanted. Also, I can't repay you enough for picking up for me at the coffee shop."

"I got your number and this date. It's more than enough to repay me."

"Oh, you're welcome."

"On that note, are you still paying for the outfits?"

"Hahaha, of course I am."

Giovane brings me to a local bakery to buy dessert then to a nice park to enjoy it at. Together we eat on the grass while we enjoy the lights in the park.

"Thank you for the great day, Giovane."

"Thank you for enjoying it with me, Lilith. Hey, do you mind if I tell you a secret?"

"I don't mind. What is it?"

"Those rumors about me being one of those gluttonous sinners…is true."

"What?"

Giovane takes off his eyepatch and sure enough, there's a mouth where his eyeball used to be in his right eye. Gluttonous sinners usually have mouths where one of their eyes used to be because they're said to always look at the objects of their desire with lust in their eyes. He really is one of them…

"See?"

"…I see."

"It's been so hard not to give in to sin that I was told to find a friend to confide in. Can you please help me?"

"I-ah!"

He's tightly hugging me, and I can feel his tears on my face.

"Please, help me. I can't do this on my own."

"Okay, I'll help you."

"I can't do this."

"I'm here for you now. Don't give up."

"No, I can't…keep up this act."

"Huh?" He's pinning me to the ground by holding my wrists. I can't slip my hands from out of his grasp. Gluttonous sinners are said to get stronger with every sin they commit and when they're committing a sin. "I'm here for you, Giovane! You don't have to do this!"

"But I want to do this. You don't understand. This was a setup from the beginning. I wanted to increase my powers through sin and what better way than to lie to a gullible girl, break her heart, and turn her into what I am."

"You can't! There are people in this park. You'll get hunted down and killed."

"I've been doing this for a while. I have friends in high places that will cover my tracks. Furthermore, I'll be sinning more by making you embarrassed and feel abandoned. No one can help you and no one will."

"Wait! Stop! Someone help me!"

"Keep screaming and crying like that. It just makes me more powerful. While we're at it…"

"Ah! Stop!"

He's tearing apart my clothes! As if this couldn't get any worse. I don't even want to know what he's going to do next. He's going to ruin my life and the plans I have for it if he bites me. I'm still struggling to free myself, but I don't see anyone around me. I could've sworn there were more people in the park. Please get help! Don't leave me like this! He's trying to bite me now! I can feel his mouth on my neck and the saliva coming from it as he licks my neck with his long tongue.

"I'll be sure to make this painful for you. Let me hear you scream."

"No! No, no, no!"

I scream louder than I think I ever have because of the pain his bite is giving me and in the vain hope that someone will hear me. It's over for me now. My life might as well end. I can feel my body go numb as my screams become quieter in my ears even though I don't think I'm screaming any softer. Please, let this be the end…

Chapter 2 – The Daily Life of a Sinner

I can see light. Did I really die? Huh? I feel like I'm lying down naked on something cold. My arms, legs, and neck are restrained! Where am I?! I look around me and see people standing around me.

"W-who are you people? Where am I?" I ask.

"That's not important for you to know, Lilith," I hear a voice say. I can't tell if it's a man or woman.

"Is this a hospital? Listen, Giovane is a gluttonous sinner. He-"

"We know what he did. No one else saw."

"There were people in the park that had to see us! They-"

"No one else saw."

Who are these people?

"What do you want with me?"

"You're a new sinner like the rest of us so you should know the rules."

"I know all about you."

"Oh? Do you know about all of us that are in the government, the Church, and society?"

"N-no, I don't."

"Then listen closely. You can join us and indulge in sin to get whatever you want in life. You could also live life as a penitent sinner with the help of the Church, but I'm sure based on what we know about you, that you wouldn't like that life. These are the only two options that you have."

"Why are you telling me this?"

From Sinner to Saint: Clawing Up to Heaven

"Just so you know the rules and that you know which side you should join. Your life is going to get harder from here and we can help you get what you want. Your comfortable life with riches and a nice gentleman to spend it with. There are several suitors here who may or may not come to you."

"You're a bunch of perverts."

"Sinners need to sin. Remember what I told you and with that, we'll let you go but not before showing you what happens if you try to rival us like Giovane."

"Uck!"

A buzzsaw comes out from the center of the table that cuts through my chest. It hurts more than the bite Giovane gave me, and yet, I don't feel like I'm dying the way I did before.

"Gluttonous sinners like us are more durable than humans. The more sin you commit the more you'll be able to endure pain such as this. After I activate the buzzsaw as a pseudo-anesthetic, you will wake up in your apartment

with a generous check, letter, and eyepatch so you

remember what happened and who you can turn to for help.

Goodbye, Lilith."

"H-hold on. Isn't there an easier way to do this?"

"This is the easy way."

"Wait!"

The buzzsaw activates and I scream until I pass out

from the unending pain. Was that all real? Sure enough just

as the person said, I find a five-hundred-dollar check, letter,

and eyepatch next to my bed to remind me of everything

they said along with what I had on me last night and some

addresses to meet them at if I'm interested in joining.

There's no way I'm going to do that especially after what

they did to me. I'm not even going to cash the check they

gave me. They can go…ugh. It feels like there's a fire in

my head. Oh, that's right. The sins of a gluttonous sinner

manifest on them.

From Sinner to Saint: Clawing Up to Heaven

I have to see what I look like now. I can see through both my eyes. Does that mean that I don't have a mouth in one of my eyes? Going into the bathroom, I find that my left eye has a mouth in it. I can see through it despite it. I check my teeth and find that I have a set of sharp triangular teeth on one side of my mouth. After checking that, I check my stomach to see if the buzzsaw left a scar and it appears that it didn't. Dang it, a scar should be the least of my concerns.

What am I going to do now? This condition just made my whole life more complicated than it needed to be. Also, why am I so hungry? I guess it's because it's still early in the morning. What's strange is that no matter how much I eat I can never feel satisfied. I have to eat way more than I usually do to get any kind of satisfaction. No, wait! It's my condition! I'm not going to be a glutton and not going to get upset! I'm going to work and try to stick this out until I get used to it.

Huh? Taking a look at the time and day, it's a day after my date with Giovane. I call work and find out that a "friend" told them that I was in an accident and wouldn't be going to work that day. While heading to work, I get unfriendly stares from people and it doesn't get better when I arrive at the coffee shop. For the next few days, fewer and fewer people show up because they see my eyepatch and the bandages around my neck. My boss then fires me the next day because my condition has made it harder to work the same way I used to, and I lash out because of the stress.

Now without a job and a condition that makes it hard to get one, I don't know where to turn to. I've been denying myself whatever seems sinful and I can hardly get any relaxation from life. TV shows, music, and games aren't as entertaining. I can hardly get enough sleep. Eating my favorite dinner feels as satisfying as eating dry crackers. The only thing that does bring me any pleasure is sin and I know when I've sinned when part of my body feels like it's changing. I don't want to be a monster. I don't want to lose my humanity, but I don't want to live this kind of life.

There's only one more option left for me, the Church. They're the only people that can heal the effects of sin. It's a wonder that they don't have more power than they should, but I guess it has to do something with the gluttonous sinners that are in power. I haven't been to a church in years so it's awkward for me to go in one again. There are some people here like me with eyepatches either on one or both of their eyes. They wait in line at the confessionals, so I go in line to wait with them. Some confessions take a minute or two while others seem to take forever. Come on, I don't have all day!

A girl behind me says, "Don't give in to the sin of impatience. It's only going to make things worse."

"Oh, thank you. I haven't been to confession in a while."

She then hands me a pamphlet that lists various sins on them.

"You might need this then."

"Thank you."

Wow, I might as well give the priest this entire list since I committed most of these sins. When I go into the confessional, I tell the priest my sins in the way that it says to on the pamphlet and mention what happened to me yesterday since I feel like I have to tell someone. He then absolves me of my sins then tells me to meet him after confessions are done for my penance. I guess I have to stay then. Right now, I feel my condition getting better with the ache in my eye going away. After waiting, the priest comes to me in a pew and I see that he has an eyepatch like me. The shock must show on my face because he pats my shoulder before saying anything.

"Peace be to you," he says.

"And, uh, to you too."

"Surprised to see another sinner like you being a priest?"

"Yes, but I guess I shouldn't be. They seem to be everywhere now that I've been turned into one."

"You've always been a sinner. You're now awakening to the manifestations of your sins."

"Did the punishment have to be so severe? I can't enjoy anything like I used to. My life is destroyed. Everything I planned is ruined. My job is gone and I'm on the edge of losing all the money I have."

"The only way God can get into some hearts is to break them. You lacked Him in your life, so this is His way of getting in."

"I guess I should feel grateful."

"Don't be so dismissive of this great act of grace and mercy. Use it to become a better person. If you need a job, there's always work that the Church can hire you for."

"I'll take the job. It's not like God is giving me any other opportunity."

"Believe me when I say that I was like you before becoming a priest. If you need someone to talk to, I'll be here. There are also the other volunteers if you think they understand you better."

"Sure."

The priest then tells me the place I'm working at and the duties I'll be doing. He also gives me a choker with a cross on it. He says that it's something that helps me keep away from sin while also hiding the bite scars on my neck. Even though it may show people that I'm a penitent sinner, I'll wear it if it helps. Plus, it kind of looks cute. Today, I'm going to be working as a chef serving at the poor house not too dissimilar from my old job at the coffee house. It's not too hard except for the cocky people I meet. I deal with them the same way I deal with the cocky people at the coffee shop, but this gets me pulled aside by one of the people I work with.

"Did I do something wrong?" I ask.

"You shouldn't be snarky even to the people who are…difficult."

"Why shouldn't I?"

"Because it's wrong. You can't repay evil with evil."

"It's not evil. Correcting a person for their behavior is an act of charity, isn't it?"

"The way you did it wasn't charitable. You don't know what those people might have been going through, so it's important to be as gentle as possible especially when you're reprimanding them."

"Okay, I get it."

From then on, I hold back my cocky remarks and try to walk back my responses when they slip out. Despite this, I'm still told to confess this. I just confessed yesterday, and I need to go back again. Since I have to go back for what I said, I guess I have to mention me looking at certain people with disgust and not so nice thoughts in my head about them. This goes on for two days until the priest tells me to do gardening work for the exact amount of pay as serving. I'm not making much as is. Maybe they'll give me more if I sin less.

Gardening is easier to do even if it is exhausting. At least I'm not dealing with any aggravating people. After work, I find a letter in the mail without a sender address. I have a bad feeling I know who this is from. The letter simply says, "Are you happy with life?". I'm fine the way I am though I'm not sure if they know exactly what I'm doing. It doesn't help that just knowing about them makes me feel like someone is watching me all the time with the worst intentions. Nothing interesting happens for the next couple of days as I hold out for better pay. This whole "work is prayer and penance" thing helps me control myself a bit more, but it doesn't help me feel any better. It's all hard work for little reward.

I go up to the confessor priest I talked to before and ask, "Excuse me, but do you think I could have a pay raise? I'm really struggling to get by and need help."

"How much of an increase do you need?"

"I need it to make at least ten dollars an hour-"

"Ten an hour? I thought you live in an apartment."

"I do, but I can't just live off the bare necessities."

"You're doing penance and trying to live a simple and humble life. It's a reward that's invaluable."

"Well, it doesn't seem to be a life for me."

"Take the value of yourself a peg down or two or it will ruin you. Pride is a terrible sin to fall into."

"My value of myself is right where it needs to be."

"Then you need some time off to reevaluate that. Take the weekend off and come back on Monday. You won't be receiving your pay for today."

"Fine."

The other people I work with try talking to me, but I walk past them without listening to what they have to say. They're no different than the priest. The penitent sinners may like me however they don't understand me. I hardly talked to them when I worked with them and they did try to be friendly to their credit. I'm just not as "perfect" as they are, so we can't relate to one another. This entire situation has me stressed out of my mind. I need to take off the edge somehow, but I can't afford to buy anything too expensive.

I still have the check from before. I wonder if they'll notice if I cash it. I wonder if it's a sin to accept money from them. Hopefully not. With the check cashed, I go to a bar-restaurant for a few good drinks and big dinner that I deserve for all the hard work I did. That was great. I might've spent two-hundred and eighty dollars on dinner because of how much I needed to feel filled, but it was worth it. That couldn't have been a sin if it stopped me from losing my mind.

Huh? Someone I haven't seen before is on the floor of my apartment. It can't be…I'll follow from a distance to see what they do. He stops by my door and waits around just as I feared. It could just be him waiting around for a neighbor, but I'm not going to take a chance, so I turn around and hide around the corner to wait him out. This probably isn't a good plan. I don't know how patient this guy is and if someone else is-someone else is coming up the stairs!

To avoid them, I go up the stairs to see where they're going to go and see another guy go to my floor and go near my room. That's not good. Ah! I think they might've seen me looking at them. They looked this way and might've seen me. What am I going to do now? Okay, okay. Panicking is definitely not one of the things I'm supposed to do. Alright. The safest thing to do is to walk out of the apartment and come back in a couple hours. Okay? Okay-Ah! They turn the corner and pin me against the wall by grabbing my throat. They were so fast, and I didn't hear them!

"How?!" I say out loud.

"Sin can give you many abilities if you just give in, and it seems like you have," one of them says.

"I didn't do anything."

"You cashed the check. That was a smart move. It's the first step, but of course, the second step is your call. Come to this place if you want to take it."

"Hey, watch where you're putting your hands!"

The guy puts an envelope in between my breasts.

"I can do whatever I want. Don't take this personal. It's just business and for appearances."

"Do you really think you can do this in public?"

From Sinner to Saint: Clawing Up to Heaven

"If we got rid of the people who saw you in the park, what makes you think we won't vacant this entire building?"

"Tch. You're horrible."

"I'm my own man, master of my own destiny, and you can be too if you join us. It's all up to you."

The man then let's go of my neck and the two walk away. I take the envelope out of my breasts and open it in my room. There's a check in it for a thousand dollars and a business card for a nearby club. It has the words, "Ask about the wine" written on the back of it. Is this some secret code or something to get into the exclusive part of the club? Hmm. I know this club. It's not like a strip club or anything like that so maybe it's fine to go to. I'm going to check it out tomorrow when it opens just to see what it's about. Nothing more.

As I enter the club the next day, I see nothing but normal people here. I'm assuming that the sinners are in their secret room. Makes sense since they are usually

separated from the public so that a fight doesn't start

between them.

I go up to the bartender and ask, "Hello, what kind

of wine do you have?"

"We have the most exquisite kinds that I doubt you

will find anywhere else. Would you like me to show you to

our wine bar?"

"Yes, please."

The bartender motions for another bartender to take

his place as he leads me to a back room then to a guard

who's standing in front of a hallway near the offices. The

bartender nods to him and he nods back as he goes back

and the guard motions for me to follow him. I follow him

into an office then to a secret hallway activated by a hidden

button underneath a table. The hallway leads to a place

where I see all the sinners are. They're partying and having a good time with nothing sinful going on from what I can see.

"There she is!" I hear a familiar voice say. The man from yesterday approaches me as the guard goes back to where he was. "I'm glad you took the opportunity. Most people take a week or more to decide on whether or not they want to come."

"I'm just here to check it out. That's it."

"I understand and I won't pressure you to stay. Enjoy yourself as much as you want because this part of the club never really shuts down. Why don't you come and sit with me and my friends? You don't have to worry about talking to them. We appreciate the company of people like us."

"I don't know. I hardly know you."

"We have drinks and food if you want. It's all on me."

"If you're offering, I guess I'll accept."

I join the man and his friends at his table that seems like it's big enough to fit everyone in this portion of the club. These people practically have a buffet of food and drinks on the table that everyone is picking from with servers coming in and out from the kitchen to replace the quickly emptying trays, alcohol, water, and soda. It all smells and looks very good, so I take some and begin to eat. Before I know it, I've already had two platefuls of food and I'm eating a third with some wine.

"Good, huh?" the man from before asks as he sits next to me.

"Yeah. I haven't eaten this good in a while even though I did treat myself yesterday."

"It's better than Giovane's food too I bet."

"I don't remember and I'd rather not."

"I get it. I'd rather not remember eating people too."

"What?"

"Oh, they didn't tell you? Giovane mixed in the flesh and blood of the people he killed into his dishes so he could sin more. Oh! He also mixed in excrement in his dishes as well."

"You're going to make me lose my appetite. Why are you telling me this?"

"No reason. I'm just wondering why he chose to spare you when he's maimed and killed every other victim of his."

"Maybe to sin more."

"Probably, but you won't find anyone like him among us. We indulge in enough sin to keep us sane while not going overboard so we keep our good looking human appearance, you get me? There are even people here from the church that come to let loose every now and then."

"Isn't it a sin to do that? Doesn't it make our condition worse?"

"Do I look like I have a fake shell on me? You can feel for yourself if you doubt me."

"I'll pass. You look normal to me."

"That's right because I know when to stop before going too far. We know our place and keep to ourselves. Can you really call that a sin?"

"I guess not. I don't know."

"What's the matter?"

"I'll have to lie in the confessional and the priest I know if I keep coming here."

"What are you going to lie about? This isn't sinful. If you think the church isn't good for you, then stop going. Here, I was told to give you this check if you came along with another place I frequent. There's a thousand and five hundred dollar check in here. That should be enough money to live off of until you make your decision. I'm not very good at convincing people and if you're going to listen to anything that I have to say, then listen to your heart. It'll tell you the right decision to make."

"Okay. Thank you."

"Any time. Now, enough with this. Let's get back to enjoying ourselves."

For the rest of the day, I enjoy the company of sinners like me that seem to know what I'm going through and agree with the way I think. We eat, drink, and dance until late at night when I decide to go back home. Monday comes around after spending the weekend with the other sinners I decide to go to work and talk to the priest and tell him that I found a new job over the weekend that suits me.

"That's great news, Lilith," he says.

"Yes, it is."

That was easier than I thought.

"Before you go, do you have something that you need to get off your mind? You seem like something is weighing you down. Do you need to go to confession?"

"N-no. I didn't commit any sins over the weekend."

This condition is killing me. My tongue feels like it's growing. Am I lying to myself?

"I trust you, but I know how sinners like you can be, so how about you confess what's ever on your mind, and if it isn't a sin, it isn't a sin. You'll receive a blessing along with it so it's not like you're going to be wasting your time."

"Okay, if you insist."

I tell the priest some of the stuff that bothers me without mentioning what I did over the weekend. He blesses like always after confession, but now I feel that my tongue really starting to change, so I make sure that he doesn't see it when I leave. This place ain't right for me. I didn't sin, or rather I didn't do anything wrong. Is there a difference between sin, evil, and doing wrong in my mind anymore? It doesn't feel like it.

Chapter 3 - Drunk on Depravity

This is the right decision to make. I don't need to go to confession since I haven't sinned at all. My condition hasn't even worsened since I started working at the club. In fact, I've never been happier in my life. I'm living in a better apartment with better clothing, shoes, and makeup to better show my natural beauty. I also have supportive friends who understand me better than anyone else I've known. Working here the past few weeks has really helped me cope with my condition. I'm finally on the path I want to be on in life.

Because of my hard work, I've been promoted to work at another club that's a bit more than the last. The people dress more risqué and dance on stages, but it isn't a strip club! I also have to dress in a similar manner to fit in. It doesn't bother me though it does get the attention of other sinners who like to flirt and try to invite me for some "fun". They have their good intentions, but it's not for me and they understand. I think they do at least.

They have harder drugs and alcohol over here than at the other place I worked at. The stuff is good especially since my condition lets me endure the negative effects better, however, the best thing about this club is that the pay and food are better. My condition has worsened a bit though the benefits of working at the club outweigh the negatives. Three weeks of working at the club get me a meeting with the boss for a promotion.

"Your hard work and dedication is paying off and turning heads, Lilith," my boss says.

"I live to please."

"I'd be careful saying that to your new employers. If you think this is a bit much, then they'll really cross the line. It's nothing sinful of course."

"I get it. To each their own."

"Exactly, but I just wanted to give you a heads up. They won't be offended if you chose to stay here."

"It's a tempting thought to stay since I love working here, but I shouldn't let a good opportunity go when it's presented to me."

"Thatta girl. I'm proud to have you as one of my workers, but back to business. Here's the kind of outfit that they want you to wear as your 'uniform'."

My boss puts on a tub top and short skirt.

"This is pretty revealing especially the skirt."

"It's no more revealing than what you have on. Your shorts are shorter than the skirt anyways."

"Yeah, but you can't peek up it see my underwear…or lack of it in some cases."

"Hahaha, you won't have to worry about people getting touchy with you. There's a strict rule that kicks out anyone who touches someone who doesn't want to be touched though there's also a rule that can get you paid a little extra if you don't mind a few grabby hands."

"I'll think about it."

"I know that you'll make the right choice. Before you go, can I get one last hug and kiss?"

"Of course you can." I give my boss a hug and kiss and he uses the opportunity to touch my butt. "You troublemaker."

"Haha, you know me. Don't forget that you always have friends here if you need anything."

"I won't forget."

When I get to the next job, I see that's it's a really sleazy place despite all the glitz and glamor of it all and it being uptown. I work at the bar and everything seems so different with how lewd people act in here. I'm pretty sure I can hear people having sex in the back or it could just be the music. Either way, this is a lot to get used to. My condition is worsening because of everything that I'm experiencing, but I can handle it. I need to calm down and get used to-!

"Hey!" I say to a guy who touches my breasts while I'm not noticing.

"Shh, don't be so loud. I'll pay you five thousand upfront if you let me touch you until you leave."

The man then takes out five thousand dollars and puts it in front of me.

"Five thousand? Hmm."

"I promise it's only just touching and nothing more."

"Hmm. As long as you don't get too touchy."

"Deal."

With that, more people come around to pay to touch me. I work more as the people's plaything than a bartender. The other people working here get the same kind of treatment then go to the back room with some people for…whatever reason. I don't want to think about it or let it get that far. Over the week, I accrue a fortune because of all the tips I get for being touched. I bring this to my new boss and ask her how much of a cut she wants.

"Hahaha. You're something special, Lilith. Very few of my workers ask if I want a cut of their massive tips," she says.

"Okay? What does that mean?"

"Because you thought about me, I'll take fifty percent and give you your paycheck. Usually, I take sixty percent and don't give them their pay for working when they don't tell me they collect tips. Most if not everyone ends up like this. Congratulations on not being one of them."

From Sinner to Saint: Clawing Up to Heaven

"Thank you, madame."

"Keep working hard and that next promotion will be around the corner."

She tells me to work and I'm hardly doing anything other than serving some drinks and drugs while being touched all the time. I don't think I need my choker with a cross on it anymore, so I wear a golden chain necklace with some golden bracelets. Not sure why I want to wear these other than they make me feel better. The people at the club notice my new accessories and compliment me on them telling me that they like me better with the gold than the cross. Part of me feels like someone from the Church sees me doing this and is reporting this to the priest. Maybe it's my guardian angel. Whoever it is, they can think what they want.

I know I'm doing the right thing because of how happy it's making me. After two weeks of working at this club, I start touching people back. Sure, I may touch people back in lewd ways, but it's nothing serious even though some ask me to go in the back for double their tip. This is where I draw the line. Most are fine with me denying them, though a few can be a bit "pushier" when I deny them. These people are kicked out of the club.

It takes five weeks of working here and being touched day in and out for eight hours a day to get my promotion. The next place I work out is more out of the way than the others. It's still in an uptown area, however, I have to go underground after confirming my identity to two checkpoints of guards. What's so special about this place that they need…Oh. I don't even want to describe what I'm seeing, nor do I want to see or hear it. Dang it, I have to work in this. What have I gotten myself in to?

As I walk into the club and make my way to my station, I keep my head down and away from what's happening around me. It's going to be incredibly hard to work with my head down and trying not to let what's happening around me bother me. Hopefully, it's worth the thirty dollars an hour. Once I get to the bar, I start working and am almost immediately forced to look up by a familiar friend. It's the man who showed up at my old apartment and gave me the invitation to work at the clubs. His name is Bryson and he's one of my best friends.

"Hey, what are you doing here, Bryson? I'm surprised to see you here," I try to say in a calm and happy way with a smile on my face.

"I'm not as surprised as you are. You are always trying to move up in the world."

"Sorry I didn't tell you I was going to be working here. I was going to tell you after the first day like always."

"I understand, but is something the matter with you? You didn't seem to notice me in front of you and you're always looking down. Is someone giving you trouble already?"

"No, not at all."

"What's the matter then?"

"It's just that…this is all a bit much for me, which is why I'm surprised to see you here since what you like is tame compared to it."

"It doesn't hurt to be risky every now and then. I do it to keep things fresh. You should keep your eyes up. Trust me when I say that it's okay to look at it. If you think what everyone is doing behind me is messed up, then that's your opinion but it ain't a fact. Come on, Lilith. Your other jobs have been preparing you for this. You can trust me."

I look up and around at what's around me. It's more messed up than what I've seen on the internet in my curiously sick teenage days. Sex is one thing, but fetish sex is another thing especially when sinners like me are doing it.

"Heh, are-are you sure I didn't accidentally enter a torture porn studio?"

"Our condition allows us to do things that would kill normal people."

"I can see that. At least it's all consensual, right?"

"Mostly."

"What?"

"It's none of your concern. I can help you get used to this."

"How?"

"Come with me."

"I'm working right now."

"I'll tell them I'm borrowing you for a second. They'll think it's one thing, but don't worry about it."

"Okay, if you say so."

Bryson then makes me watch lots of different sexual acts in a room for hours until closing. It's an…eye-opening experience.

"Well, Lilith, how do you feel now?" Bryson asks me.

"I feel. Great actually. Better than I ever have as a matter of fact!"

"I'm glad. Oh, hide your gaping mouth eye before you go out in public."

"Thanks for reminding me."

Gapping mouth eye? When I get home and remove my eyepatch, I see what he's talking about. My entire left eye has become a mouth now. Along with this change, my mouth has sharper teeth that look like a vampire's teeth especially with the four in the front while my long tongue remains the same. I like this look. I may get some hate for it, but I've learned that you either take the hate or let it overwhelm you. I'm going to embrace it and become the best sinner I can be.

This club is even better than I thought. It not only has the best drugs and alcohol in the city, but it also has the best entertainment that I'm paid to watch. My paycheck gets me everything that I want and the tips I get for letting people touch me and walk around semi-nude all add up to an even better apartment.

During one of the private shows, a friend of mine asks, "So, do you want to try what they are or something more dangerous?"

I consider it for a second before smiling and saying, "I want my first time to be special."

"Oh, Giovane didn't…"

"He didn't. That's why I want it to be special and dangerous."

"That's our girl!"

"But it's not going to be with you."

"Ah! Denied!" the others in the room say except for our performers.

It takes me a few weeks to make my plans and decide my target, but when I find him, I feel something special in me that lets me know he's the right one for me. My target is a boy much younger than me who I find walking home from school. I take his gaze with my appearance and take him aside and flirt with him. He's in the palm of my hand especially since I give him a little peek of what his eyes keep gravitating towards. I let him take pictures of all kinds so I can always be on his mind. I give him a kiss then send him on his way. His blood-red face and the way he's acting tells me that he's madly in love with me.

We go out together for a week before I can no longer hold back what I want to do to him. On one date, I bring him to one of the hotels run by a sinner I know and aggressively cuddle him, to say the least. He says no, no, no, but I know he means yes, yes, yes. His tears are the most delicious part of him besides his cute expression and his blood that I taste. I keep using him as my little toy until I feel satisfied.

"That was amazing. You are such a good boy toy," I say as I lick his face.

From Sinner to Saint: Clawing Up to Heaven

Huh. He seems knocked out. I might as well admire my work while I'm at it. What the? What's happened to me? There's a mouth on my left breast, my arms have turned into tentacles, there's an eye where my belly button was, all of my teeth are razor-sharp, I have a weird red collar and restraints made of blood where my golden chain and necklace were, and there's a mouth where my crotch used to be. Looking into the mirror, I see that my right eye has turned pitch black and there are three horns on my head along with a red-eye in the center. Hold on. What did I just do? What have I become?

Chapter 4 – Clearing the Fog of Wickedness

What did I do? How did I ever think was okay? I

did what Giovane did to me in a worse way. Not only did I

turn him into a gluttonous sinner like me, but I also…I

don't even want to think about it. Wait, is he still-okay,

okay, he's still alive. That's the only positive in this

situation. That and me finally seeing what's become if this

can be called a positive. I look like a whorish monster

because of what I did. I need to get to the priest for

confession! The church is always open to sinners like me so

From Sinner to Saint: Clawing Up to Heaven

I should be able to make it there as long as I stay hidden. If

people see me, then they'll know I did something wrong.

That could lead to me getting arrested or killed by a mob in

the streets.

To not attract any attention to me, I go out of the

window. Okay, this may not be a good idea. The jump to

the next building looks farther now that I'm here, and I'm

not sure if I can make it. These tentacles should give me

some extra reach, so maybe I can. I jump up higher than I

think and land on the roof of the building. Wow! That was

better than thought. Maybe these abilities aren't so-No! I

can't let this power get to me.

Even though I don't know where the church is, my

new eyes allow me to see almost everything around the

city. I can even see through nearby objects like the floor.

The horns on my head feel tingly as I can listen in to what's

ever close to me. I can even hear the conversations on the

streets level as if I was down there. I can't play around with this too much so I head in the direction of the church while ignoring as much of the noise and the temptation to stay like this as I can.

As I leap from rooftop to rooftop, I can hear everything from sounds of violence and cries for help to romance and talks about politics and business. It's no wonder why gluttonous sinners want to sin more if sin gives them this power. No, get my mind off this! I can hear someone running and leaping from rooftop to rooftop like me. Is it another sinner like me? Does someone know what I did? I better keep running.

They're close to me now. They're people in black robes and custom masks with intricate designs. Are they vigilantes that hunt down sinners like me? Are they sinners like me that want to convince me to join them?

"Leave me alone!" I scream to them.

I have to get away! I have to get help! Ah! They're shooting projectiles at me with their hands! Ah! They got me as I was jumping across a rooftop! I've fallen all the

way down to a dark alleyway and landed on the street level.

I'm okay, but I'm not sure if that's good because I'm

surrounded.

"What do you want from me?" I ask them.

One of them steps forward and says in a deep voice,

"You have no reason to fear us, Lilith. We're your friends."

Another one slightly takes off their masks and says,

"It's me, Lilith."

"Bryson?"

"We've had a friend follow you after you said you

were going to make your first time special. After they told

us what you did and what you became, we knew that you

truly belong with us."

"I'm sorry for the deception, Lilith. You were given

promotions quickly to boost your ego and as sin for the

bosses to profit off of. They thought you would end up like

one of the slaves for the comfortable life of wealth with a

powerful man that you've always wanted, but you did something unexpected. I'm proud of you."

"I guess I shouldn't be surprised that you were in on this too, Bryson!"

"Before you get mad, you should hear our offer."

"I'm done with all your offers and promotions! Look at what it's turned me into!"

"We can hide that with prosthetics. We can make you the best looking fake body you've ever seen. Better even than the real one you had before."

"We are offering you a position among the elites, Lilith. You will be at the top of the world like you've always wanted."

"I don't want anything! I want to be human like I used to be!"

My tentacle arms reach out when I hold them out and they impale two people before they are cut off by the people around them. My legs are then shot at by the projectiles that come out of their hands before I can make my escape.

"Calm down, Lilith. I don't want to hurt you anymore."

"You'll see how good things are when we bring you to your new home."

"Stop! Get away from me!"

A new group of masked and cloaked people descends from the rooftops as a bright light blinds everyone for a brief second. This new group attacks the other as one of them stands over me. Is that…

"Are you okay, Lilith?"

It's the priest from the church I used to go to. His appearance looks like of a sinner like me with small blades coming out from his arms that look like blood red crystals. His left eye is crimson red with a black cross in the center.

"If you can call this okay. I'm sorry for doing this to myself."

"You can confess it all at the church, but first we have to get you out of here. Can you move?"

"Hardly."

The priest motions for someone to come down and they land on the ground and fly up into the air and land on the rooftop. A small group along with the priest then escort me to the church where I confess everything that I did. Surprisingly enough, they don't harshly reprimand me with anything other than a penance of working hard with them again. It's enough to bring me to tears as I feel my appearance start to change. I'm mostly back to normal now with a few wounds where my mutations were. I'll have to wear bandages until they completely heal and go away. The church then throws a celebration for my return. It's small but nice.

While eating, I ask the priest, "So, how come you never told me about that group of yours?"

From Sinner to Saint: Clawing Up to Heaven

"Because you're not a sinner like some of us were. God let us keep some of these deformities for a reason."

"Is there any way I can help you?"

"Not with what we do because your deformities are gone."

"I'm actually thankful for that. I'll do the best I can at my job and whatever other help you need around the church."

"Your help is appreciated. Thank you."

"For what?"

"For coming back."

"Oh, please. Don't make me cry again."

For the next couple of days, I help the church by working at the poor house and by giving them a portion of the money I earned from my previous jobs. This helps to improve working conditions and the conditions of the buildings. While running out to get lunch for the people I work with, I come across a police scene at the tallest building in the city. People are talking about this building belonging to a gluttonous sinner and sure enough, a monster appears at the top of the building.

I can't find any words to describe this monster other than it being an amalgamation of sin. Gunfire can be heard even from here as the monster tries to fly only to plummet to the ground. Everyone scatters as it falls. The monster then happens to splat near me. We then slowly go near it to see if it's still alive. It lifts its head as its eyes suddenly concentrate on me. With its broken limbs, it reaches out to me.

From Sinner to Saint: Clawing Up to Heaven

"Lilith…please, help," it says in a voice that sounds masculine and feminine.

Wait, I remember hearing this voice when I first woke up as a sinner. This is the one person who was talking to me back then. I remember them. So, this is what I was going to turn into if I didn't repent. What a pitiful thing.

"All that worldly power and wealth can't help you in the end, can it? If I was you, then I'd ask God for forgiveness while you still can," I say before turning away from it.

Another surprise happens a couple days after that. The priest tells me about a new sinner like us coming to work at the church. I go to meet them and it's…it's the boy I…

"Don't be shy, Lilith," the priest jokingly says.

"I'm not shy! It's just that…I don't know if I have any right to talk to him."

"It's okay. He's forgiven you."

"What?"

The boy comes to me with a soft smile on his face.

"Hi, Lilith."

"H-hi."

"You look more beautiful now than before."

"I don't think I deserve your compliment after what I did to you."

"It's okay. I forgive you."

"You say that so easily. Do you really?"

"I do, and I'm here to ask…um, do you still want to be my girlfriend?"

"Huh?"

"I'm also responsible for what happened, so I'm going to take responsibility for it and our baby."

Someone in the church that I work with says, "Your what?!" in shock before being quieted down.

"I don't even know if I'm pregnant yet."

"Still. I want to make things up to you."

"That's sweet of you."

"So, what's your answer?"

"Maybe we can be together. I'll think about it."

He hugs me as the priest smiles, laughs, and shakes his head as he walks away. I hug the boy back and wonder if he's really the right one for me. I guess it wouldn't mind because of how brave he is for coming to me like this and going down the route I did. Hopefully, this isn't the sinful part of me talking and making excuses to be with a younger boy to fulfill any lingering fetishes I have.

The End

Little extra!

Since this story is inspired by *Tokyo Ghoul* by Sui Ishida. I

drew the Kaneki meme with Lilith at work because I

thought it would fit and be funny.

From Sinner to Saint: Clawing Up to Heaven

Behind the Story

- As mentioned in the extra picture, this story is inspired by the *Tokyo Ghoul* manga by Sui Ishida.

- At first, I was going to include a part about the gluttonous sinners wanting to eat human flesh as part of the *Tokyo Ghoul* inspiration, but later didn't think the story needed it.

- I tried to make the cover and chapter images in the same style as the *Tokyo Ghoul* manga covers.

- I got the idea for this book after watching the *Tokyo Ghoul:re* anime with my mom.

- The image of the monster in the last chapter was meant for a fifth chapter of the book, but I ended up combing the fourth and fifth chapter like I usually do, so I threw it in where the monster appeared so the image didn't go to waste.

- I didn't plan to imply an older woman/younger boy relationship at the end of the book. You can either assume they got together or didn't, if you want. I didn't want the boy to be a loose thread in the story and this is the best way that I thought to tie it up.

- Mouth eyes are very common in my books especially in my Choice and Consequence series.

- I didn't want to call the main character Lilith, but it's the only name that stuck with me for her.

- Just like the previous story, sin is shown to be something that takes something away from you. In this case, it takes away your humanity.

- Another thing the book is meant to show is how sin will make you commit other terrible sins if you aren't careful and repentant.

- I was going to have a chapter based on Lilith's first time working with the Church, but discarded the idea after thinking that Lilith wouldn't care too much about it either especially since she couldn't relate to the people in it.

Sheep in Wolf's Clothing
Be Perfect
Or
Perish
Trust
in the
Pious

Chapter 1 - Piety in an Unlikely Place

"I'm sure this will be enough to pay for your cooperation, Mr. Wyatt."

Not really, but what choice do I really have?

"Yes."

"Thank you for your compliance. Have some time off while you're at it. You seem to be shaken."

"Thank you. You're too kind."

"You're welcome. Go and be perfect."

"I strive for it every day."

Or at least I try to, especially in front of people like this. Working down in the mines day in and day out is supposed to help me achieve perfection with how taxing and humbling it can be. It's a low paying job with the highest reward being the sweat and tears that are meant to cleanse our souls. I like most others believe in the God we worship, but the Pious pride themselves on their perfection that they say they've earned from Him. The Pious live in their city that some believe to literally be made of gold because of how it looks and the gold mines beneath them.

Those who aren't Pious live outside of the bright city and in less than ideal conditions let's say so that we may be humbled and perfected through it. The mines that I work under hold treasures of all kinds that my city runs on. If we find something rare, like diamond or gold we're allowed access into the city to work as a maid or cleaner for the Pious. Nothing too good, but probably better than what we have now. If you really want to be among the elite, you need to be "perfect". This means hardly sinning or rather hardly going to confession.

The less you go to confession, the closer you are to a promotion. The fewer people know of your sins, the more attention you get from the Pious, and more likely you are to get a better job from them. This is why I was paid and given time off. They don't want me reporting the dead body I walked over and dug up to the higher-ups. I don't know who the body belongs to nor do I want to know because I either accepted their offer or I would end up as one. The only way justice can happen for the deceased is for God to answer my prayers, and He seems to be either waiting for the right moment or denying my prayers as of late.

The typical penance for a person that gets caught sinning or confess a particularly bad mortal sin is to publicly pray in itchy clothing, naked, or while being flogged. Sometimes you are required to be your boss's slave for a period of time. I've heard rumors of the sinful things that the bosses make their slaves do in private. Should the slaves refuse to do every command of their boss then it's likely that they'll end up like the body I found. It makes sense considering the number of slaves in the mine. The body could belong to a slave who died from exhaustion and the boss hid their body to hide her mistake to get closer to her promotion.

From Sinner to Saint: Clawing Up to Heaven

This whole system makes me sick to my stomach. To get around it, a lot of people and I don't confess our venial sins even though it would spiritually help us. I'm sure there are people that make excuses for their more serious sins just so they can make more money. It wouldn't surprise me if certain priests and the higher-ranking officials in the priesthood frame the sins of one person on another, especially since there are priests who will break the seal of confession for profit and promotion. The Pious control everything and there are very few of them that I consider to be good people who are trying to weed out the bad. Because of this, I have to take justice into my own hands.

Today is one of my few days off, so I take advantage of it by going to one of the many propaganda stations that the Pious use to spread their messages and teachings. To sabotage it, I've taken the tools I have from the mine, rework the wiring, and once they activate it, it blows up and falls onto a row of their parked cars. The Pious have many other stations like this, but at least it's good not hearing their constant messages in one part of the city. After, I tear down some of the Pious posters and destroy and vandalize their art. These things may be made well though they're an eyesore to me.

While doing my part to clean up the city, I hear something behind me. There shouldn't be anyone in this area at work time, so maybe it's just my imagination. The authorities that go through these areas don't always come this way because of how "dirty" it is. They won't always get people to replace and clean their propaganda because of this. Again, I hear a noise. To be safe, I check around the area then hear another noise. There's no one here. I don't even see anything on the ground that could've dropped that made the noise. The buildings around this area are falling apart so I would expect to see a part of them on the ground. Huh?! Someone tapped my shoulder from behind.

"Ye-!" I say before seeing who it is and falling down.

It's a sinner that's been locked up because of his horrible crimes. I know it's one of them because of his scary-looking clown mask, the black hole in his cracked chest, and his boots that have gold dust on them. These kinds of sinners are slaves in the gold mines to work for the Pious. I've heard that working in the gold mines is worse than working in the normal ones. This sinner is staring me down…while holding out his hand?

"Come with me, if you really want to make a difference," he says in a deep voice.

"What? Why should I trust you when your sins have made you look like a monster? I know what you are, and I should report you to be rearrested!"

"You know that wouldn't be the right thing to do."

"Why do you think that?"

"Because I've been watching you all day tear about the propaganda of the Pious. You know that these perfectionists don't have the best intentions nor God's will in their hearts, but you're going about it the wrong way."

"How? They feel the hurt that I put on them. This isn't the only time that I've done this and there's more that I've done besides destroy a tower and rip apart posters and deface statues."

"They may feel the hurt, but you make the others below them clean up your mess. I'm sure you've been forced to clean up your own messes as well."

"As long as they know that there are people out there who disapprove of their actions, it's fine with me."

"I've been down the same road you're on. It's not worth it."

"What makes you think you know me?"

"I've worked in the mines before. I used to cause all kinds of mischief with my friends and family until we got caught. Some got executed. Others were given the same torturous treatment I was given, and now, none of them are alive. You know this to be true. You know that the Pious treat everyone unfairly for their own gain."

"Okay, what do you suggest that we do?"

"First, take my hand and get off the floor."

"Right." I look at his hand for a second and consider again whether or not I should join him, but then again, having help is better than no help, so I take his hand and get off the ground. "Okay, so what are we going to do now?"

"We're going to go join the others."

"The others like me who are against the Pious?"

"In a way. They are others like me."

"Other escaped sinners? This is going to be interesting."

"I'm glad you think so."

Chapter 2 – Virtue and Pompousness

Sinners like this man with the clown mask that I'm following are a rarity to see. The black wires and closed tubes on his back are there so they have to rely on their master for food. There's also supposed to be a device on their back that instantly kills them if they leave their work area. It's a wonder that this guy is even alive let alone a group of people like him. Part of me wants to report him while another wants to believe him.

He could be telling me what I want to hear so I can join his group or worse. I'll just have to wait and see. Despite his deep voice, he sounds honest. I wonder if I used to know him since he said he worked in the mines. I've seen dozens of people try to start a revolt or protest in the mines but end up getting arrested and never being heard from again.

From Sinner to Saint: Clawing Up to Heaven

As we move through the shadows and hidden alleys of the city, I ask the man, "We never exchanged names. My name is Wyatt. What's yours?"

"Oh, yes. My name is Terran. It's nice to meet you, Wyatt."

He's polite and gave up his name to me. He has to know that if I told the authorities his name and what he was doing then they would trust me and arrest him. Maybe he is being honest with me. We keep making our way through the alleys until we see a protest happening in the streets. Terran slows his pace as he watches it and tries to listen. Through the cracks in the building that we go through, we see people holding up crosses and pictures of people that I assume to be loved ones as they chant prayers and against the Pious. This crowd is taken out by gas then forced to strip and be whipped in the streets as an example to all.

"Don't let it bother you, Wyatt," Terran says as he picks up his pace.

Albert Oon

Maybe you should take your own advice. His
footsteps sound heavier so maybe he's mad at hearing and
seeing glimpses of what happens almost every other day.
On our way to our destination, we make our way
underground and to a dark basement with a steel door at the
end that has a cross on it. Terran knocks seven times on the
door before it opens. Inside is a ruined church with people
inside who wear masks and have appearances similar to
Terran with very few people who like me. Churches, where
I live look, similar to this, however, there are a couple of
machines in this church that have fluids, wires, and tubes
on them. So, this is how Terran has managed to survive
though from the looks of it, they'll have to share the same
machines rather than having their own.

"This is Wyatt, the troublemaker who's been
sabotaging the Pious' propaganda and plans in the mines."

"I'm a troublemaker? I'm sure you've caused your
fair share of trouble too, Terran."

"It's good that you're here, Wyatt," one of the masked people say. I don't think I'll get used to their deep voices.

"I'm here because you guys are against the Pious, and I'm assuming that you have some kind of plan that's better than what I've been doing."

"Much better."

"Well, tell me what it is."

"We're going to free the sinners like us from the gold mines."

"We're going to do what?! What makes you think we can even pull that off?"

"We have a cave that was dug out by the first one of us who managed to dig their way to freedom and an insider in the city. We also have a mystic who tells us that it is God's will that these sinners should be saved now."

"Of all the things we can do…"

"What do you think we should do? You know every other option there is doesn't work."

"But is this really God's will?"

"You'll have to trust us on that."

"You guys look like you can barely keep yourselves together. Besides, they'll replace the slaves we take. Do you know how many people bang their head on the golden gate to the city to live in there even as a slave? People walk over each other when that gate opens to make it inside."

"We trusted in God to deliver us from our slave masters and now we trust in Him when we're given another purpose. Don't you trust Him?"

"Tch, I do."

"Then it's decided. We head out in two hours."

"Why two hours?"

"It's the time we were given by the mystic."

"Fine."

From Sinner to Saint: Clawing Up to Heaven

For two hours, I keep to myself and repeatedly clean and check my tools. The sinners talk to themselves not about what we're going to do, but their sins and how to avoid doing them. Keeping away from sin is important, however, it's not the most important thing to consider right now. I look around and see someone who looks like the mystic they were talking about and he's a sinner like them, mask and everything. He looks like he's praying, which is what we're going to need. I say a couple prayers as the time comes.

We head into a tunnel near the church that has lamps that light the way. There are many footsteps that go along this path so this it's been used quite often. I then see many tunnels that must've been used for their escapes and trips back and forth.

Still unsure of the plan, I quietly ask Terran, "Do we have a plan for the guards?"

"Most are out because of the celebration happening in the golden city. We shouldn't come across many."

"But what do we do if they discover us?"

"Run for it. We were told by the mystic to be as quick as possible."

I think I'm less confident about this plan now. Regardless, the head sinner reminds us where we're supposed to go, the groups we're in, and what each group is going to do. I get teamed up with Terran and together we go through the mines and free the slaves we come across. It's surprisingly empty in here for a place meant to be full of slaves.

Curious about this, I ask Terran, "There aren't that many slaves this way. Maybe we should head in a different direction?"

"All the slaves secretly were told they were going to escape today if they came to work. Most laughed at the idea, even the moles to the Pious disregarded this news.

From Sinner to Saint: Clawing Up to Heaven

Since today's a celebration in the city, the slaves were given an option to take the day off. The ones who doubt us are in the city probably part of the celebration or resting in their cells."

"Oh, I see."

I don't blame the slaves for doubting their escape. Working here is Hell on earth or rather beneath it. Since there aren't many guards here and our pace is casual, I take some of the gold I find in the mine. Wouldn't hurt to use it for later. Once we free the last slave on our determined path, the ground starts to shake and the supports of the mine break apart. We rush to the exit only for me to drop my gold before we get to it.

"Why were you carrying gold with you?!" Terran asks.

"Why not? It's free!" I answer.

The tunnel's entrance collapses.

"There goes our way out! Now what?" I ask.

"We have to take the normal way out. Thankfully, I know that way. Let's hurry and leave the gold behind!"

"Okay, okay!"

We hurry to the exit and into the golden city for my first and last glimpse of it as I watch it collapse. The golden buildings, streets, and statues fall as the ground beneath them crumbles. Debris from above seem to selectively fall on cars and people as if God were choosing to kill certain people with the debris. I see someone who is stuck in the ruins of a flying car. I move to help them only for a helicopter to crash into the car. Okay, I get the message, God!

Terran, I, and a few others manage to make it out the only entrance of the golden city as it falls down. When we and the people around us look into the crater, we can barely see the tall buildings that were seen from miles away. A lot of the buildings look like they're still intact so maybe there are still people alive down there, but I don't think we have anything here to get to them. The weight of the city collapsed the mines that were constantly being dug out and expanded. The Pious' pride literally made them fall. If I would've kept the gold I got, then I would've fell with the city. Now I understand the true weight of sin.

The End

Behind the Story

- I accidentally gave a little red tint to Wyatt's dirty boots on the cover. I used this accident for the story to show how the Pious deal with their enemies and what they're willing to do to keep their sins a secret.

- At first, this story was going to be about a little girl who was being chased/protected by a large monster man in a clown mask. Once she realized that he was protecting her, she set out to clear his name with him. This book's theme of the Pious and seemingly perfect people being unholy compared to the repentant sinner would be played by the people in government and some people in the Church. I might still write this story later with some changes and adjustments if I get the right inspirations.

- Terran's clown mask is inspired by Needles Kane from the *Twisted Metal* video games.

- Terran has one hand that's black as you can see on

the cover. This was meant to be a part of his past sin. His hand was cut off because of who he killed with it. Similarly, in the first version of this story, the monster man killed people with his hands and his hands were deformed in the experiments done to him.

- Here's a draft version of the cover that I drew at work in my free time.

- This story is different from the previous two in that it is meant to show how sin can be prevalent even in those who claim to be holy.

- This is the draft version of this paperback book that I made at work at the same time as making the Sheep in Wolf's Clothing draft cover.

From Sinner to Saint: Clawing Up to Heaven

If you liked these stories, then check out these other ones!

Everyone sins, but it takes real strength to repent and change for the better. In the three stories included in this collection, each of the characters has something that's preventing them from becoming the person they're meant to. They will face many challenges and horrors while trying to overcome their pride on top of it all. Sainthood can only be obtained through hardship as these tales can either end in Heaven or Hell.

Love is the Ultimate Weapon Against Sin

In these three short stories, love finds a way to overcome evil.

Love burns away the sins of the past. Love ends wars and

destroys hatred. Love is more valuable than anything in the

world and can change it. Find out how love does this in this

collection where love is the ultimate weapon against evil. This

book collects; The Spark of World Burning Love, Revenge First,

Love Later, and Love Against the World along with Behind the

Story extras that detail what went behind each story.

THE MONSTER AND HIS MISTRESS

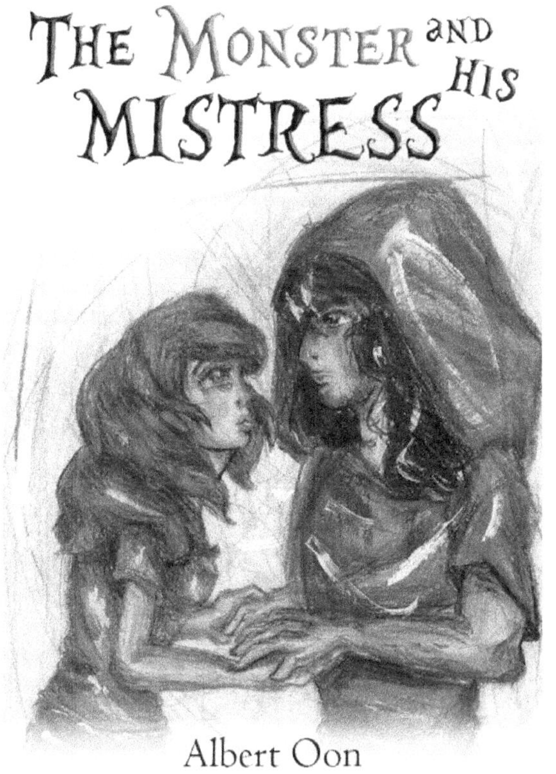

Albert Oon

A tyrant is given another chance at life and his queen follows along to make sure he's doing the right thing and happy. The two will embark on a journey that will make them face small to larger than life challenges. Their love for each other is strong, but is it strong enough to last until a tyrant can be redeemed? Find out in this epic fantasy, romance story. This version of the story includes a short prequel story and behind the scenes extras after every story.

Kyrie is a girl who's been used as a living sex doll for most of her life. Now her mother and she have outlived their usefulness. Her mother is killed while she is left for dead in a forest. Her guiding light is her only means of salvation in this dangerous forest. Zita is a woman who's lived a life of comfort and degeneracy thanks to her spoiled upbringing. She's mysteriously trapped in her room with two choices; grow up and take responsibility for her choices by facing several challenges or do nothing and suffer forever.

From Sinner to Saint: Clawing Up to Heaven

Check out these free eBooks on Smashwords too!

Collected in this special book are eight stories that are distinctive of Albert's style. Five are inspired by songs, one is inspired by a dream, another is a scrapped story brought back for this special book, and the last is a prologue for an upcoming book. This book covers; romance, fantasy, and horror so there's something for all audiences in this collection of weird and unique stories.

After being severely punished and abused by a vigilante group, Vera is thrown into the sewers beneath the city. These sewers contain sinners who are viler than the muck they inhabit with everyone out for themselves. The only way out is down through the sewers so Vera begins her descent down to escape and to possibly find redemption for her actions.

From Sinner to Saint: Clawing Up to Heaven

A hundred people every year fall into a near-death state with no rhyme or reason to it. Rosanna searches for the reason why and ends up in a dimension where killers and people affected by tragedy attack her. She must play by the dimension's rules to escape or else she could be trapped in this sadistic game forever or until she surrenders her soul to it.

Albert Oon

In Albert Oon's 90th book and final Choice and Consequence

story, a young boy named Michael is kidnapped, sexually

abused, and beat for the pleasure of a mistress. He is freed from

a satanic wedding by an act of God and is now in Hillside City.

The psychological damage of his past and abuses reaches its

peak as he faces his demons in his mind along with the

consequences of his previous actions.

Check out my blog, Albert Oon: Behind the Stories, for free short stories, free book samples, song/poem attempts, and more! Follow me on Twitter, Facebook, Instagram, and LinkedIn to see what I'm doing next.

www.ingramcontent.com/pod-product-compliance
Lightning Source LLC
Chambersburg PA
CBHW052014150726

47999CB00004B/1661